COLI THE CATERPILLAR

in 'Graze'

By

T.N. CRAWFORD

AuthorHouse™ UK
1663 Liberty Drive
Bloomington, IN 47403 USA
www.authorhouse.co.uk
UK TFN: 0800 0148641 (Toll Free inside the UK)
UK Local: 02036 956322 (+44 20 3695 6322 from outside the UK)

Because of the dynamic nature of the Internet, any web addresses or links contained in this book may have changed
since publication and may no longer be valid. The views expressed in this work are solely those of the author and do
not necessarily reflect the views of the publisher, and the publisher hereby disclaims any responsibility for them.

Any people depicted in stock imagery provided by Getty Images are models,
and such images are being used for illustrative purposes only.
Certain stock imagery © Getty Images.

This book is printed on acid-free paper.

ISBN: 979-8-8230-8845-9 (sc)
ISBN: 979-8-8230-8847-3 (hc)
ISBN: 979-8-8230-8846-6 (e)

Library of Congress Control Number: 2024912604

Print information available on the last page.

Published by AuthorHouse 06/24/2024

authorHOUSE

Colourful flashes, light up the gloom,
among the flowers, butterflies zoom,
with an artistic hue,
from a palette of blue,
swirling around a meadow, in bloom.

Tucked away, in behind an old wall,
hidden from view, they are really small,
from the outside, a hedge,
but under the leaf's edge,
are eggs stuck safely, so they don't fall.

Coli the caterpillar hatches,
from dozens of eggs, laid in batches,
doing nothing but eat,
he will need all those feet,
as he leaves behind big, bare patches.

Within an army, Coli did march,
stepping in unison, as they arch,
segments, suckers and hook,
is an interesting look,
as he chomps his way, through the green starch.

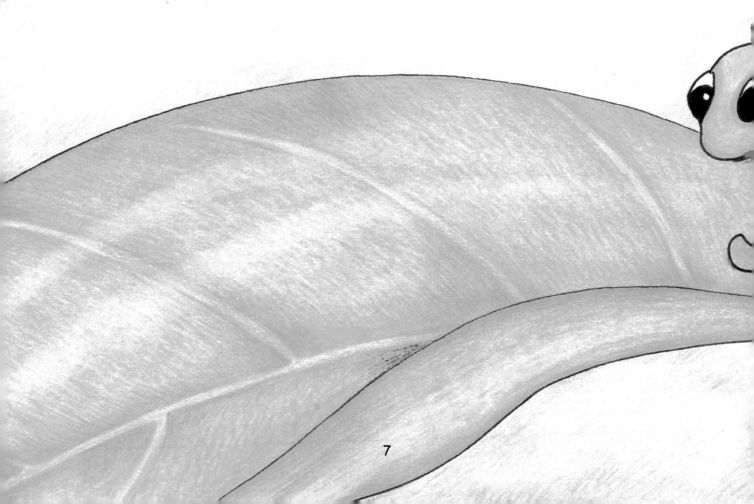

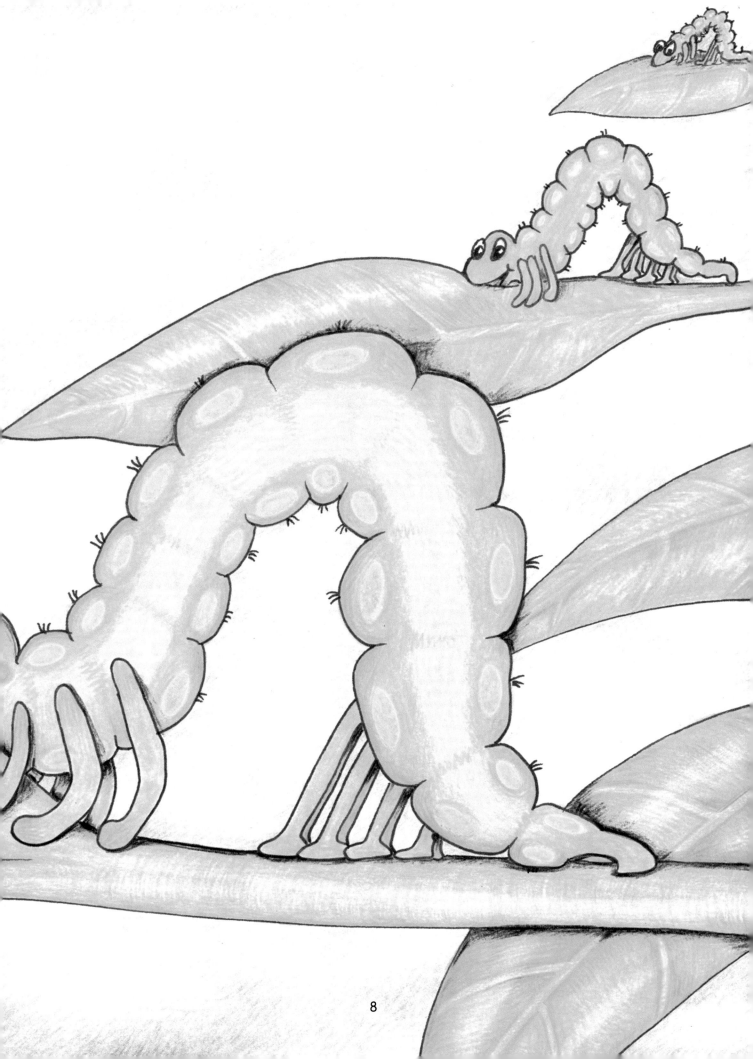

A slug was afraid to cross the trail,
Coli made him look like a sick snail,
as blackbirds like to eat,
juicy slugs as a treat,
and luckily, their trick didn't fail!

Wriggling away, across the land,
suddenly, all the leaves tasted bland,
by losing some features,
he'll join different creatures,
as Coli 's size begins to expand.

12

Caterpillar's lives, are just a race,
and with changes, about to take place,
turning from green to brown,
while he hangs upside down,
as he spins himself a silken case.

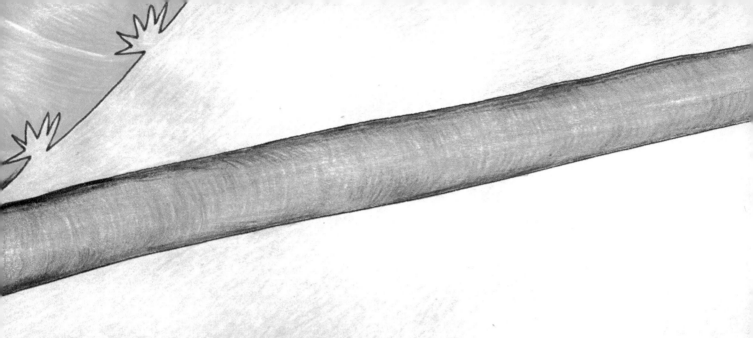

Coli was secured by a tether,
as the warm sun dries it like leather,
waving 'Bye' to the slug,
being snug, as a bug,
inside, he's cosy from the weather.

Coli emerges, completely new,
from his cocoon, this butterfly grew,
with his tongue, in a curl,
it's easy to unfurl,
sipping the nectar, then off he flew!

18

Coli missed his friend, who was slimy,
he followed the tracks, that were shiny,
from under the hedge row,
was the gooey fellow,
growing up they were not so tiny!

20

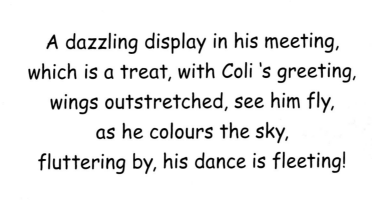

A dazzling display in his meeting,
which is a treat, with Coli 's greeting,
wings outstretched, see him fly,
as he colours the sky,
fluttering by, his dance is fleeting!

Printed in the United States
by Baker & Taylor Publisher Services